THE ROAD TO BETHLEHEM

BRIAN WILDSMITH

OXFORD
UNIVERSITY PRESS

It was spring, and God sent the angel Gabriel to Nazareth to visit a young girl called Mary.

'You will have a son,' he said. 'His name will be Jesus and he will be called the Son of God.'

Some time later, Mary and her husband Joseph had to go to Bethlehem. As it was a long way, Mary could not take her cat and dog with her, so she left them with a neighbour to look after.

The cat and the dog missed Mary very much. So one day they ran away
to try and find her.

On their way they met a fox. He was stuck fast in a rabbit hole. Cat and Dog wanted to help him, so they pulled and pulled until Fox was free.

'Oh, thank you,' said Fox. 'Where are you going to?'

'To Bethlehem to find Mary.'

'Can I come too?'

'Yes, just follow us,' they replied. And off they went.

On their way they met a goat. He had got stuck in a cart while trying to steal some carrots. Cat, Dog, and Fox all wanted to help him, so they pulled and pulled until Goat was free.

'Oh, thank you,' said Goat. 'Where are you going to?'
'To Bethlehem to find Mary.'
'Can I come too?'
'Yes, just follow us,' they replied. And off they went.

On their way they met a bear. He had been
caught in a hunter's trap while trying to steal honey
from a bees' nest. Cat, Dog, and Fox all wanted to help
him, so they pulled and pulled until Bear was free.

'Oh, thank you,' said Bear. 'Where are you going to?'

'To Bethlehem to find Mary.'

'Can I come too?'

'Yes, just follow us,' they replied. And off they went.

They came to a big palace and there they met three camels.

'Where are you going to?' said the camels.

'To Bethlehem to find Mary.'

'We'd like to come with you,' said the camels. 'But we have to wait here for our masters.'

'Perhaps we'll meet again,' said Cat, Dog, Fox, Goat, and Bear. 'Goodbye.'

As they came near to Bethlehem, they met some sheep, grazing in a field.

'Where are you going to?' said the sheep.

'To Bethlehem to find Mary.'

'So are we. We know the way. Just follow us.'

When they reached Bethlehem, they could not see Mary in the inn.
Instead they found her in the stable with her new-born baby.

Mary was delighted to see Cat and Dog and their friends.
'Come in,' she said, 'and meet my baby. His name is Jesus.'

Then the three camels arrived, carrying three kings.
'We have followed a shining star,' said the kings. And kneeling down,
they offered the baby their gifts of gold, frankincense, and myrrh.

'Our journey is ended now,' said Cat and Dog. 'We have found Mary and
her baby Jesus, who is the Son of God.'